TALES
OF
SESAME GULCH

TALES OF SESAME GULCH

written by Ruthanna Long • illustrated by Tom Cooke

FEATURING JIM HENSON'S MUPPETS

A SESAME STREET/GOLDEN PRESS BOOK
Published by Western Publishing Company, Inc.
in conjunction with Children's Television Workshop

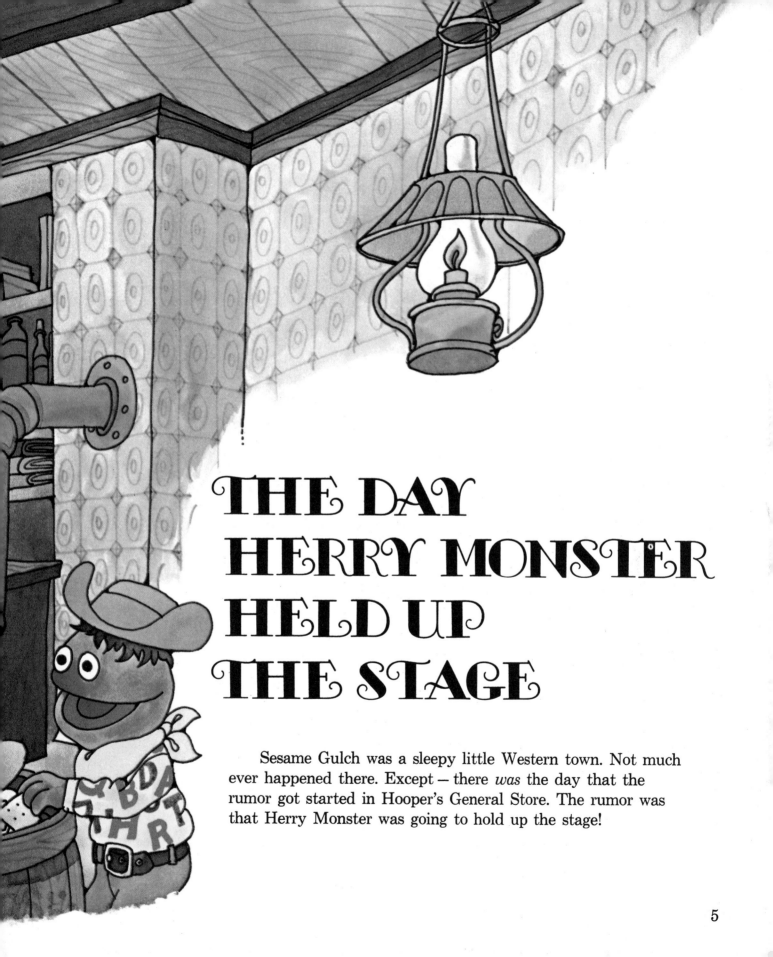

THE DAY HERRY MONSTER HELD UP THE STAGE

Sesame Gulch was a sleepy little Western town. Not much ever happened there. Except — there *was* the day that the rumor got started in Hooper's General Store. The rumor was that Herry Monster was going to hold up the stage!

The Alphabet Kid heard every word that the grownups
said about Herry Monster, and hurried out to spread the news.
He was headed for the Sheriff's Office to tell the two famous
lawmen, Sheriff Bert and his loyal sidekick Fearless Ernie,
when he ran right smack into old Ernie himself!

"Guess what!" the Alphabet Kid said. "I just heard that
Herry Monster is gonna hold up the stage at Hootenholler Pass!"

"Thanks, Kid," said Fearless Ernie. Then he wheeled and
strode toward the Sheriff's Office, with the Alphabet Kid hot
on his jingling, jangling heels.

Sheriff Bert sat at his desk thumbing through a dog-eared J.C. Pigeon catalogue.

"Guess what, Bert!" said Ernie as he came in the door, still followed by the Alphabet Kid.

The Sheriff looked up. "What is it, Ernie?"

"Come on, Bert. *Guess!*"

"I'm not interested in guessing games today, Ernie," Bert said seriously. "This is an important day."

"Why, Bert?" asked Ernie. "What's special about it?"

Bert looked over his shoulder at the clock.

"Today," he said, "my *pet pigeons* are arriving on the stage! It's due any minute. So let's get moving!"

For the first time, Fearless Ernie looked a little worried.

"Well, uh, Bert . . . I don't think we need to be in such a hurry."

"What?" yelped Sheriff Bert. "You *did* mail in my order to the J.C. Pigeon Company in St. Louis, didn't you, Ernie?"

"Sure, Bert, but . . ."

"Then today is the day my pigeons are coming in on the stage."

"That's just it, Bert. The stage is going to be a little late."

"LATE? Why is the stage going to be *late*, Ernie?" shouted Bert.

"Because," answered Fearless Ernie, "Herry Monster is going to *hold up* the stage."

"Oh, *no!*" shrieked Bert. "Well, don't just stand there letting the grass grow under your boots, Ernie. Go round up a posse!"

"Sure, Bert," said Fearless Ernie, and moseyed out the door.

8

Ernie stood on the steps of the Sheriff's Office and looked down the main street of Sesame Gulch. He saw a number of leading citizens of the tiny town, going about their business.

"Hey, everybody!" he called.

They all stopped to listen.

"Herry Monster is going to hold up the stage. So let's get up a posse and get over to Hootenholler Pass!"

Marshall Grover, who had just ridden into town, strode over from Franklin's Livery Stable.

"That is absolutely right, Fearless Ernie," he said. "Do not fear! I, Marshall Grover, and my Wonder Horse, Fred, will accompany you!"

"Me, too," said Big Bird, who was standing nearby in the street, practicing fancy rope tricks with his lasso.

9

In a matter of minutes the brave citizens of Sesame Gulch had formed a posse to head off Herry at the pass. They galloped off in a cloud of dust.

On one side of the narrow trail through Hootenholler Pass, the dangerous desperadoes and Herry Monster were hiding behind rocks and bushes, lying in wait for the stagecoach.

On the other side of the trail, the posse hid behind more rocks and bushes and lay in wait for the desperadoes.

The sun was high when they all heard the rumbling of horses' hooves and stagecoach wheels on the rocky trail. But they heard a louder rumbling, too — the sound of 500 stampeding cattle!

"Hey, Bert," said Ernie from behind a mesquite bush, "here comes a stampede!"

"Oh, no!" Bert groaned, peeking out from behind a big boulder. "Oh, no! Not today! Not the XYZ Ranch's annual cattle drive North! Those cattle are going to stampede right in the path of the stage! Somebody do something!"

"Oh, my *goodness*!" exclaimed Grover. "Look at all those *cows*!"

The stagecoach and the charging herd of cattle raced toward Hootenholler Pass.

"They'll never make it!" cried Bert. "They're going to crash!"

"It looks like it, Bert," said Ernie.

"I cannot watch," said Grover, covering his eyes.

Suddenly, Herry Monster jumped out from his hiding place and leaped astride the narrow, rocky pass. Quick as a wink, Herry swept up the stagecoach and hoisted it high over his head as the XYZ cattle thundered underneath.

"Look, Bert," said Ernie. "Herry Monster *held up the stage*!"

"Look, Ernie!" replied Bert. "My *pigeons*!"

15

As Herry set the stagecoach down gently on the trail, a cheer went up from the Sesame Gulch posse. But the Jinx Gang was not cheering.

"When I said to hold up the stage, *that's* not what I meant!" the leader of the gang shouted at Herry. Then she and the boys jumped on their horses and galloped toward Texas.

But Sheriff Bert didn't notice.

"My pigeons! My pigeons are flying away!" he cried.

"They're not flying *away*, Bert," said Ernie. "They're flying home — back to the J.C. Pigeon Company in St. Louis. They're *homing* pigeons, Bert."

For Fearless Ernie and the rest of the brave posse, things soon got back to normal in Sesame Gulch. Even Bert was happy because the J.C. Pigeon Company returned his pet pigeons on the next stage. Herry Monster received a brass belt buckle from Wells Fargo in honor of his brave deed. And the Alphabet Kid never forgot the day that Herry Monster held up the stage.

17

19

BONANZA!

Along about sundown, Cookie Monster hurried down from the hills into Sesame Gulch. He scurried by Hooper's General Store. Then he disappeared around the corner.

"Oh, my goodness!" said Grover. "Cookie Monster was in a *very* big hurry!"

"That's right," said Big Bird. "He didn't even say hello."

Bert looked thoughtful. "But he did say something."

"Yeah," growled Oscar. "He said 'BANANAS!'"

"I thought he said 'cookies'," suggested Ernie. "Didn't you, Bert?"

"I don't know, Ernie. He *always* says 'cookies'!"

Rodeo Rosie lassoed the hitching post. "Well, never you mind what he said. What I want to know is — what is he up to? Where's he goin' in such a hurry? What's in all those little brown bags he's totin'?"

"Maybe some terrific trash!" guessed Oscar.

"Or maybe some birdseed?" asked Big Bird.

"Those bags look like the bags prospectors carry *gold* in," said Bert.

"Gold?" said Ernie.

21

"GOLD?!" they all shouted. "There's *gold* in them thar hills?"

Suddenly, Cookie Monster flashed past them again, racing back through Sesame Gulch.

"After him!" shouted Rodeo Rosie. "He'll lead us to the gold!"

They ran down the street to the end of town, but Cookie Monster had already disappeared into the foothills. "I knew we'd never catch him," grumbled Bert.

"Never mind, Bert," said Ernie, pointing to a trail of cookie crumbs in the dust. "We'll just follow this trail of cookie crumbs."

"Good idea!" exclaimed Rodeo Rosie. "After him, boys!"

They followed the cookie-crumb trail through arroyos and over mesas, past sagebrush and cactus. Finally, just before sundown, they stopped on top of a ridge to rest.

"I knew this would never work," said Bert. "It's getting dark. How can we follow the trail?"

"Hey, everybody . . . *look*!" said Big Bird.

They all looked over the ridge, and there, nestled in the rocky foothills, was the yawning opening of an old mineshaft. As they watched, Cookie Monster trudged out of the mine, pulling a loaded mining cart behind him.

"Look, everybodeee!" cried Grover. "We found the gold mine!"

"Gold?" said Ernie.

"What gold?" asked Bert. "There's no *gold* in that mine! Those are cookies!"

"Cookies?" said Ernie.

"COOKIES!" they all shouted, rushing down to the mine.

MARSHALL GROVER MEETS THE (GULP) NOON TRAIN

As Marshall Grover rode into Sesame Gulch one morning, he heard the Count calling to him from the telegraph office.

"Good morning, Count," said Marshall Grover. "Have you read any good telegrams lately?"

"Yes, I have," said the Count. "As a matter of fact, I have read five good telegrams already this morning. And, only a moment ago, I read one fascinating telegram addressed to *you*. Listen to this: 'Meet the noon train — or else!' The telegram is signed 'M'!"

Marshall Grover took off his white hat and mopped his brow with his white bandana. "Or else?" he said. "What does that mean?"

"I don't know," said the Count.

"Signed M?" asked Marshall Grover. "Count, does the telegram explain who M is?"

"How could it explain?" cried the Count. "The telegram has only six words. Look. I will count them for you. 'Meet' is one word, 'the' is two words, 'noon' is three words. Ha, ha, wonderful, wonderful. 'Train' is ..."

"Thank you, Count. It is very nice of you to count the words for me," said Marshall Grover. "But right now I have another problem. I do not know anyone named M."

"Well, there are many people whose names *start* with M," said the Count. "M could be Mean Mary, the rustler. That is one person. M could be Mad Montana Max, the bank robber. Ha, ha, that is two people whose names start with M. M could be the Mysterious Masked Bandit. Ha, ha, that is three, three M's! Wonderful, wonderful. M could be ..."

"Please, Count," said Grover. "All those M's sound very (gulp!) scary. I do not want to go alone to meet a very scary M." Grover pulled out his pocket watch. "It is now eleven o'clock. The noon train will be here in one hour. Will you go with me to meet (gulp!) M?"

"No, I cannot," cried the Count, "and there is one very good reason why I cannot. The good reason is . . . counting. That's it! I have to stay here and count the words as they come over the wires." He spun around and vanished into the telegraph office. The door slammed shut behind him.

"Well, that is a good reason," said Grover. "I will find someone else to go with me."

OUCH!

From a distance came sounds of hammering, and muffled cries of "Ouch!" and "Oh, my goodness, I did it again!"

"Big Bird!" said Marshall Grover. "Of course. Big Bird will go with me." He hurried down the street and into Luis's Harness Repair Shop.

Big Bird looked up from the saddle he was trying to fix. "Oh, hi, there, Marshall Grover. Did I hear you calling my name?"

Oh, my goodness, I did it again!

"Yes, Big Bird," said Grover. "I have received a very exciting telegram. Listen to this: 'Meet the noon train — or else! Signed M'."

Big Bird gasped and dropped the tack hammer on his foot. "Ouch!" he cried. "That smarts!"

"Oh, my goodness!" said Grover. "Now, as I was saying, I have received this very exciting telegram and I thought it would be fun if a bunch of us got together and went down to the depot to meet..."

Big Bird was shaking his head very hard. "Oh, I don't think so, Marshall Grover. I mean, I have so much to do right here. I really don't have time. Busy, busy, busy," he muttered.

Marshall Grover looked at his pocket watch. "Well, it is only eleven-fifteen," he said. "I still have forty-five minutes to find someone who will go with me to meet the noon train."

31

Marshall Grover set off down the street toward the Livery Stable. "I will ask Oscar to meet M with me. Maybe that is something a Grouch would like to do."

Oscar was in his rain barrel by the stable door. "I heard that," he shouted. "Oh no, not me. I'm not going to meet any stupid train."

"But, Oscar," said Marshall Grover. "I thought you were my friend."

"Listen, Grover," said Oscar. "Friendship is a two-way street. So you stay on your side of the street, and I'll stay on my side. Okay?" The lid of Oscar's rain barrel slammed shut.

Marshall Grover looked at his pocket watch again. "Oh," he gasped, "it is eleven-thirty. Only thirty minutes until noon. I must hurry and find someone who will go with me to meet (gulp!) M."

33

Right across the street, Ernie and Bert and a bunch of cowpokes were lounging in front of Hooper's General Store.

"Ernie and Bert!" exclaimed Marshall Grover, hurrying over to Hooper's. "My good friends Ernie and Bert. Surely they will not let me down."

"Ernie and Bert!" he cried. "Guess what! I have wonderful news. M is coming and we must all hurry down to the depot to meet the noon train."

"Right!" said Ernie. "I do have to hurry — but not to the depot. I have to hurry home. I just remembered that I promised Rubber Duckie I'd give him a bath this morning. So long!" He lit out in the direction of the 123 Ranch.

"Gee, that reminds me," said Bert. "I have to hurry and feed my pigeons." He rushed off in the other direction.

"And we have to hurry and poke some cows," mumbled all the others. They ran to the hitching post, jumped on their horses, and galloped madly in all directions.

"Hey! Are they scared?" gulped Grover. He looked at his watch. "Fifteen minutes before twelve!" He mopped his forehead with his bandana and looked around wildly. "Will nobody go with Grover to meet the noon train?"

Suddenly, there came the sound of galloping hooves, a cloud of dust, and a hearty, "Whoa, there, Silver!" Prairie Dawn, Pony Express Rider, galloped up Main Street and slid to a halt in front of Hooper's General Store.

"Howdy, Marshall Grover," she hollered, leaping off Silver and shouldering the U.S. Mailbags. "How's everything?" But before Grover could answer, Prairie Dawn had disappeared into the store with the mail.

"Prairie Dawn is very brave," said Marshall Grover to himself. "She would not be afraid to go with me to meet (gulp!) M."

In a moment, Prairie Dawn came racing out of Hooper's General Store with the new sacks of mail. She threw them over Silver's back and leapt into the saddle.

"Wait, Prairie Dawn!" called Grover. "Please stay and go with me to meet the noon train."

"I heard all about that telegram ya got," said Prairie Dawn, reining in Silver with one hand. "There's nuthin' I'd like better than to go with ya to the depot and give that lowdown sidewinder M a piece of my mind. But I'm carryin' the U.S. Mail, and the U.S. Mail must go through. Neither snow, nor rain, nor M on the train shall stay this Pony Express Rider from her appointed rounds. Giddyap, Silver!" she cried. They whirled around and were gone.

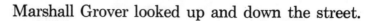

Marshall Grover looked up and down the street.

No one was in sight. Dust hung thick in the air from the sudden departures of his friends.

There was no sound of a friendly voice, no hammering from Luis's Harness Repair Shop, no clinking of soda glasses in the General Store. Only a shutter somewhere flapping in the wind, and the rustle of the tumbleweeds rolling down the empty street.

Then ... far off ... but coming nearer, he heard the mournful whistle of a train, the (gulp!) noon train.

Marshall Grover looked at his watch. "Five minutes before noon!" he cried. "Oh, no. I must go to the depot all by myself."

He pulled his hat brim down low over his eyes, tucked his thumbs into his belt, and marched bravely down to the depot.

SESAME GULCH

Grover stood alone on the creaky platform, his heart pounding beneath his badge, his feet shaking in his boots.

The train came chuffing slowly down the line and stopped with a screech and a sigh. Great clouds of steam rose from around the wheels. Grover looked at his watch. It was exactly twelve noon.

Marshall Grover pulled off his bandana and mopped his brow as he waited for the passengers to get off. He waited, and he waited. "Hey, maybe M missed the train!" he said.

Suddenly a big carpet bag bounced down the passenger car steps and landed, THUD, on the platform at Grover's feet. A pair of silver-toed boots stepped down from the train. "Oh, there you are," said a voice. Grover gulped and slowly looked up. There, right next to him, stood . . .

"Mommy!" cried Marshall Grover. "Mommy, Mommy, Mommy! M is for Mommy! Mommy is a person whose name starts with M! Oh, Mommy, I am so glad to see you!"

"Hello, there, Grover," said his Mommy. "I see you got my telegram."

"Oh, yes, Mommy, I did," said Grover. "But why did it say, 'Meet the noon train — *or else*?'"

"Because," said his Mommy, "I wanted you to meet me *or else* I would not have known where to get off the train."

PRAIRIE DAWN OF THE PONY EXPRESS

Prairie Dawn, the Pony Express rider, was thirty minutes this side of Sesame Gulch and right on schedule, when — over the pounding of her pony's hooves — she heard a high-pitched *wail*.

"Run for it, Silver," she shouted in her pony's ear, "or we're done for!"

They galloped round a curve. Suddenly, Prairie Dawn saw a pile of boulders ahead, blocking the road. "Drat the luck!" she exclaimed, pulling Silver to a halt. "This must be the work of Wild Willie Wailey and his gang!"

At that moment, two masked bandits stepped from behind the rocks. The tall bandit sneered and grabbed the mail pouches. The short one pointed to the hill behind them **and** said in a gruff voice, "Thataway, Pony Express. The boss wants ta see ya!"

With the tall bandit leading the way and
the short bandit walking behind to make sure she
didn't escape, Prairie Dawn led Silver up
the hill to the hideaway of Wild Willie
Wailey and his gang.

A mangy bunch of bandits was gathered around a campfire. "If this isn't the sorriest-lookin' gang of owlhoots I ever did see," Prairie Dawn muttered to herself.

She headed for the scruffiest bandit. "Are you Wild Willie Wailey, the leader of this ornery bunch of polecats?" she demanded.

"What if I am?" mumbled Wild Willie.

Prairie Dawn glared at him. "How dare you ambush the Pony Express and take the U.S. Mail?"

"Do you really want to know? Do you really care? Hah!"

"Sure I care, Wild Willie," she answered. "But you've done a terrible thing. Just think about that!" Prairie Dawn stared at the miserable faces around the campfire.

Wild Willie stomped his foot. "Okay, I'll tell you why. You never bring letters to us. You whiz by on yer fancy pony with letters for other people. But for us, the Wailey Gang, nothing. It's not fair!"

The other bandits all began talking at once. "That's right. It isn't fair. We want letters, too."

Prairie Dawn lost her temper. "Whoa, now!" she hollered. "Stop yammering. Just one dinged minute! Do *you* ever write letters?"

"Nope, I guess we don't," admitted Wild Willie. The bandits hung their heads.

"Lookie here, now," Prairie Dawn said. "If you want to *get* letters, you have to *write* letters first."

The bandits huddled together and whispered. At last, Wild Willie said, "Mebbe you're right, Pony Express. Soon as we steal some writing paper we'll write some letters."

"No more stealing!" Prairie Dawn said. "Besides, I always carry an extra supply." Reaching into her saddlebag, she pulled out some Pony Express tablets. "Here, Wild Willie," she said. "Pass out this paper to the gang."

"Sure," said Wild Willie. "Now, where kin we steal us some pencils?"

Prairie Dawn lost her temper again. "No more stealing, I said! It's wrong! Here, I'll share my Pony Express pencils with you."

Soon each bandit had a pencil. "Now," said Prairie Dawn, "get started."

The bandits got busy. At first they wrote slowly, but as they thought of things to say, they wrote faster and faster. Soon, they were chuckling over their papers.

"Well, Wild Willie," said Prairie Dawn, "I'll be moseyin' along now." She picked up the mail pouches. "I guess you won't need these any more."

"And remember," she said, "when yer ready to mail yore letters, let me know. I'll stop by for 'em and they'll ride with the rest of the U.S. Mail."

She threw the mail pouches over Silver's back, and swung into the saddle. "So long, now," she shouted, as Silver wheeled and galloped off in a cloud of dust.

And as she rode away, they heard her cry, "Neither snow, nor sleet, nor the Wild Willie Wailey Gang shall stay this Pony Express rider from her appointed rounds."